DAVEY'S CHRISTMAS MIRACLE

RHYS EVERLY

RHYS WRITES
Romance

Davey's Christmas Miracle

Copyright © 2021 by Rhys Everly

Cover Design by Ethereal Designs

Editing by Jules Robin

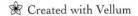 Created with Vellum

ONE

Davey looked at the choir and puked a little in his mouth. The whole sight gave him the desire to barf. Elf hats, red bows, ruby garlands, and green overalls. If you could spell "tacky Christmas" visually, the carolers would be it.

Instead of dozing off on their perfectly tuned singing, like all the holiday shoppers, he kept on, walking with purpose few had around him. Unlike all the uptight, self-serving, egotistical people surrounding him, competing for who would spend the most money on the smallest item, he had somewhere to be and work to do. He was already five minutes late, and the slow, dazed shopping stream wasn't helping.

He finally mounted the escalators, pushing through a family of fast food consumers and rolled on to his work place, John Logan. His supervisor glared at him as he made his way to a door with the word "Private" inscribed on it and a keypad on the latch.

He keyed his personal password and dumped his bag on one of the lockers, scanning his thumb to clock in, and then rushing back out where Shannon, his bubbly colleague, was waiting for him to finish her shift, impatiently tapping her foot while processing the payment of her last customer.

"You're late. Again," someone said, and at first Davey though it had been Shannon, but her lips were unmoving, smiling at her customer. He turned around and jumped as he came face to face with Emily, his supervisor, standing so close in proximity he could smell her BO.

He stuttered. "I'm sorry. You know how slow these fuckers are when shopping. Took me ages to get to the escalators." He wasn't afraid of her; he just hated confrontation.

"That's the third time this week alone, Davey. The boss isn't thrilled with your performance lately. I wouldn't give him more of an excuse to fire you," she said and walked away, the look of bitterness stubbornly painted across her face.

What a miserable bitch! Davey thought as he started up his till and greeted his first customer. Who cared about five minutes of tardiness? They had to put up with the stupidest creatures on earth:

Christmas shoppers. They should be getting paid overtime just for that bravery alone.

This day already had the prospect of being dreadful, and his suspicion was confirmed when his first customer proved to be a nuisance. He hated feeling like this, being so unlike himself, but he couldn't help it. His soul was black and his mood was blue. It was Christmas after all.

"Can I pay for these, and would you mind telling me if you have these gloves in red?"

Davey looked at the pair she was talking about, and he looked at the display shelf just behind her where dozens of red pairs were flashing a big hello to everyone who passed by.

"Just right behind you, sweetie," he gritted between his teeth. He couldn't deal with any more stupidity today.

It had started quite simply, really.

Waking up next to Sam, who had been giggling at his phone while texting incessantly. He hated being woken up before his alarm had gone off, so that fact on its own gave the day a definitive description.

After he'd shaken the sleep off him, he'd inspected closer to find Sam chatting to a dude on Grindr, and his mood plummeted. After pointless screeching, Sam had told him they never said they were exclusive, even though Davey was certain some unwritten dating handbook surely said that after three months of dating, exclusivity was a given unless otherwise discussed. Yet Sam took it upon himself to explain his need to live his life to the fullest and why he didn't want to be tied down, which only meant one thing to Davey: He was not good enough to keep a guy to himself.

A breakup later, he was now at work having to face the worst of humanity when all he wanted to do was sit and cry in his bed until the end of time.

No wonder he hated Christmas. All the crap in his life seemed to take place during the *loveliest* time of the year.

When his break came three hours later, he decided he was too hungry to digest his home-packed salad so he ventured into the chaos of the mall and grabbed a few McNothings and greasy fries to fill the empty stomach and the void in his chest.

What was it with men being unable to keep it in their pants long enough to get into a long-term relationship?

That was all he ever asked for.

He didn't want a Prince Charming. He'd given up on him and his white horse long ago. All he wanted was a guy who could stay in a relationship with him for more than two months. It wasn't too much to ask, yet so impossible to attain. In the six years since he'd come of age and out of the closet his most notable partnership had lasted five weeks and ended over what else? A text message.

He had promised himself, if it didn't work with Sam, he would quit dating for good.

What was the point of screwing men of all ages if he scared them all away? He might as well be serving pieces of his heart in a platter for strangers' consumption.

Finishing his meal, he wiped his hands in a paper towel and swore off dating for good.

From now on his penis would have the sole pleasure of fucking endless bottoms until there were no more lows to reach.

He returned to work and saw Jimmy, the boss, working in the office and decided to bug him one more time about his time-off request. He'd be damned if he worked 24/7 during December, and it was unfair, not to mention illegal, to do so.

"Hey, Jimmy," he said, knocking pointedly on the open door.

Jimmy withdrew his eyes from the computer long enough to register Davey and then resumed his work. "What can I do for you, Davey?"

"It's about my time-off," he mentioned, knowing full well that Jimmy knew what he wanted.

His boss set his hands away from the keyboard and onto the wooden desk, huffing. "Davey, it's impossible. You waited too late. It's our busiest time of the year," he said looking him straight in the eye.

"Come on, Jimmy. I'm not asking for much. Just the 22nd and 23rd off so I can celebrate with my family, seeing as I won't be spending any time with them on Christmas Eve," he nagged.

The truth was he hardly had any intentions of traveling all the way to Wisconsin to spend time with anyone he was related to, but he needed the extra time off.

He needed a breather before the craze that was going to follow. Especially now that it had all gone down the drain with Sam. He just needed some time to himself. Whether to cry himself to sleep or laugh his way through Netflix, it was too early to tell.

When he returned to his position, the lines had doubled in size, so he did his best to get rid of the ever-growing horde of impatient, loud customers. His next customer dropped a shopping bag on top of his counter, startling him. He looked up, his face full of rage ready to shoot daggers, but bit back his retaliation the moment he set eyes on said customer.

He was older, that much was obvious, but not by much. His grey eyes, spoke volumes with their sadness behind his spectacles, and there was a sprinkle of salt-and-pepper in his hair. He didn't smile, but he was staring at Davey too, greeting him with a soft voice that Davey thought didn't match his confident look.

He took the shopping cart and emptied the contents in paper bags, scanning them all one by one. His gaze kept darting back to the man's face, betraying his attraction. Maybe the guy liked him too. Maybe he would ask his name and Davey could ignore the nervous tapping of the customers behind and chat him up. Maybe Davey could get his number and they could go out. Maybe the customer was *the one*.

Davey shook his head as he passed the bags to the guy, shaking the thoughts off. That was what had gotten him into so much trouble. He couldn't keep thinking like that. It only ever ended in hurt and anguish, and he had promised himself he was done with those feelings.

The guy paid on his credit card and walked off with nothing more than an awkward smile, never looking back.

Of course he hadn't. Because these things didn't happen in real life. No one looked at anyone and thought *I'm gonna spend the rest of my life with you* and told the story of their love-at-first-sight to their grandkids.

And even if they did, it would go a bit more like "I saw him and I knew I wanted to screw his eyes out. But then he wouldn't go away the next morning, and that's how you guys came to be." Davey knew all too well how men were, and he wasn't gonna let anyone else use him and abuse him ever again.

Just as he was finishing up with the next

customer, he saw the man coming back. He had come back for Davey. To ask him out. To tell him…

To tell him he didn't take the security pin out of the scarf. No! Love in real life didn't happen like that. Love in real life didn't happen, full stop.

"Can you get the pin out of the scarf? The security guard won't let me go away," he said, frustrated.

Davey took the fabric in his hand. "Sure," he said. It was soft and fuzzy but not overly warm.

It was an item that had been brought in only this week, but it hadn't been as popular with shoppers as the wool ones. It was pink and purple. Not a great color scheme for the festive hordes but it still managed to look festive.

Davey inserted the magnetic side of the pin to the counter and removed the ink cartridge from the piece of fabric with ease. He wrapped it up instinctively and passed it back to its rightful owner. "That should do the trick," he said and smiled at him.

The guy took the scarf back, ignored Davey's smile, and fled down the escalators once again. For all he knew he was probably straight and chasing after his wife. It wasn't as if he ever crushed on gay guys. He only got in relationships with them.

At the end of his shift, and after begging his boss for the gazillionth time to give him the time off, he made his way back home, burrito in one hand and phone in the other.

He browsed through the Cinderfella app he had downloaded during his break, to look for men out and about in his proximity. Men who were available and looking for sex. After all, there was no better way to get over a guy than to get under another.

He already had a dozen messages asking him questions from "wer do u live?" to "top or bottom?" and even to "any more pics?"

He would, under normal circumstances be squeamish about men's inability to have a proper conversation before they got to the juicy part, but he had been dumped and humiliated for the last time. Therefore, he replied to every single message and awaited responses.

Some of them never came back, while others took only seconds to respond. Within ten minutes of being in the subway, he had received two invitations for "Netflix & chill," five dick pics, three hole pics, one request for a threesome with a couple, and a full gallery of a couple's bareback sex encounters.

Thankfully the train was empty, and so he was able to continue his hooking up session, discarding those he deemed inappropriate or those he simply didn't like. By the end of his journey, he had settled for a handsome Italian who had just moved to the Big Apple and was looking to experience the metropolis in all its glory. He lived approximately ten minutes away, so he wouldn't have to waste a lot of time commuting. All they needed to decide upon were the details.

As his stop approached, the guy still hadn't replied with what time he wanted Davey over, so he assumed he had either run out of power on the way home or couldn't talk.

And so he waited. He had to wash and change anyway, so he could use the time to prepare for the visit. Did he even have any condoms? Sam usually took care of the supplies.

An hour and a whole lot of preparation later, the Italian had gone missing from his app.

Bastard!

Wasting his time when he'd probably found a better looking screw for the night, and instead of messaging him to cancel, he had just blocked him.

Good fucking riddance, he thought as he threw his phone across the room onto the bed. When it bounced off the mattress and onto the floor, it pinged, and Davey rushed to check he hadn't broken the screen. The Italian hadn't messaged him back.

Instead, a new message was waiting in the app from a dude named Ave, so he opened it up and read.

Hello!

Hi, Davey replied and after hitting send, he tapped on the guy's profile to look at his pictures.

Recognition sprang through him, and he opened his mouth in awe. It was the guy from the store. The guy with the scarf. The handsome, sophisticated dude that couldn't get past the security guy because of the pin in his bag.

What were the fucking chances?

You look familiar, Ave said.

I'm the guy from John Logan. I forgot to remove the ink pin from your scarf, he replied.

Is that what it is? Huh, I never knew, he messaged back.

Who didn't know that the security pins had ink in them?

Yeah, they're meant to prevent people removing them and stealing them from the store. If you do, ink spills all over the clothes and they're ruined, he told Ave.

Thank God, I didn't remove it myself, then, he replied.

Yep.

So… how's your evening? Any plans? he asked, and Davey had already guessed where the conversation was going. Just when he'd thought he had someone intelligent to talk with, they turned the conversation to "plans."

Just chilling at home. I'm beat. You? he answered and let Ave pick up the conversation and lead it where he wanted to.

Same. Just out for a drink at the moment, but going back home soon. I'm exhausted, he said.

What do you do?

I'm a bar manager. Tonight's my only night off this week, he wrote after a minute.

Ah, so you're also initiated in the assfuckery of customer service, he replied on instinct. Whenever he met someone who worked in his industry, he always tried to get them to admit how much they hated their job.

Well, I actually do like my job. But Christmas is a pain in the ass, I'll give you that, he said.

That's putting it mildly, Davey retaliated.

The next message took time to be written and when it arrived, Davey could almost imagine the guy saying it.

Do you want to grab a coffee sometime?

Davey didn't know if he did. He had wasted himself on endless "coffees" that took him nowhere. He had wasted an endless fund of money on eating out with guys trying to determine if they were a match, only to come to the conclusion that a one-night-fuck was best.

But then again, Davey hadn't had an actual conversation with a human being, even in the form of electronic messages, in a while. Even Sam was a one-night-stand that had turned into a rushed relationship. Nothing about Sam had given Davey the spark. No one had ever given him the feeling that they would work out. He still tried, though.

Every damn time. But no one else was as willing to put in the time and effort.

Sure. When is good? he finally typed. Why the hell not? The least that could happen would be a good screw, so why not? It wasn't as if he was gonna get invested in anything. Davey had promised himself he would be a free bird from now on.

Tomorrow afternoon?

Davey didn't have to look at his work schedule to know he couldn't make it. He was starting work first thing in the morning the next day. But he always broke for lunch at twelve. He could make it work.

Only if you meet me at the mall, he replied.

Sounds like a plan, Ave said, and they exchanged good nights.

Tomorrow it was then.

TWO

The next morning, Davey woke up with an bothersome stomachache despite his good mood. He went through his morning routine casually, shaving beard and armpits and moisturizing where appropriate, but when he looked at his watch, he realized he was going to be late for work if he didn't get a move on.

He skipped the shower, hoping that deodorant would cover up his lack of cleanliness, but he doubted the date would be anything more than that with hardly an hour to spare between shifts.

He dressed quickly in the work clothes from the day before after spraying them with a generous amount of Febreze and ventured into the streets, rushing to the subway. Half an hour later he emerged from the train and was rewarded with a Cinderfella message from Ave.

He opened it as he stepped onto the escalator, but he found himself unable to continue his manual walk up the staircase. He stood to the side instead, staring at the message on his phone.

Hey, good morning. So sorry to do this, but I've been called to work early. One of my supervisors called in sick and I need to be there all day. Rain check?

Davey didn't even have the energy to go off on the guy on the other end of the app. Instead, he locked his phone and pushed it back in his pocket with only minutes to spare before he was late for work. Yet again.

Typical of men to do crap like that, and cancel plans finding stupid excuses like work. He was the fucking boss. If he wanted to, he could make it work. His boss was hardly ever behind the counter, preferring to sit in the office all day, browsing the Internet, watching YouTube and occasionally doing the necessary paperwork.

Emily was there, watching him stride in with an eyebrow raised towards the store clock on the wall. Always on his case even though the store wasn't even open yet.

All they had to do was clean out their sections, a job for those who were closing down. And yet those people couldn't bother wiping their own fucking ass after the store was closed and their shift had ended.

Other than that, he had no other prep to do since he was always on checkout duty, so he had no shelves to fill nor clothes to fold. He really didn't know what Emily's problem with him was, but he wished he could wipe that smugness off her face one day.

It wasn't as if she was any better at her job than he was. He certainly had deserved her promotion more than her, but he guessed she had an attribute he didn't: an interest in licking the boss's ego.

He dropped off his bag and mittens in his locker but kept his scarf on as he was still rather cold and walked to his station, starting up his terminal and clearing all the labels, cartridges, and paper that hadn't been disposed of the night before.

The first customer only walked in at half nine, but once they'd stepped in, it was as if they'd sung a war cry calling the demons straight from hell. He didn't get any time to breathe until he broke for lunch at half twelve.

He treated himself to a warm eggnog latte and watched the shoppers cart around looking for their next indulgence. Seeing how busy everywhere was, maybe he could give Ave a raincheck after all. Crap happens no matter how prepared one was so he decided to give the man a chance. Who knew? Maybe he would be special.

Hey, it's ok. We've been so busy I didn't break until now, anyway. Let me know when you're free, he said and hovered over the send button for a few seconds before pressing down on it.

The response came as he was going back to work. It *was* a surprise. He didn't expect a reply at all.

Pulled some strings and managed to get the evening off tonight if you're still up for it. Does 8 sound good?

Well, that changed things. Eight was no rushed date before going back to work. Eight was a date past dinner, before bed. Eight could definitely lead to sex. He needed time to go back home and shower before meeting the guy.

"Let's say 8:30 and it's a date," he responded and put his phone down as he returned to his register.

The stomachache returned and made Davey doubt its validity as an actual physical ailment. Was he nervous about meeting a total stranger whom he had only shared no more than a couple of words with in real life?

It was fine, he had to repeat to himself. Ave had messaged Davey to meet him after work, on a night out. He wasn't going out with *the one*. He was going on what was probably an A-One-Night booty call, sugar-coated with dinner. He'd seen and done this before. Everything between meeting up and post-dinner was fluff to fill in the silence while trying to estimate how good of a blow the other could give.

He should know by now that his heart was broken one too many times and there was no hope anyone would actually take the time to put it back together. That was how *fiction* worked. Real life was a whole other deal. A rawer, more animalistic deal.

Men were driven by their sex drive and not by any internal compass. Once they got what they hunted for, because God forbid they weren't hunters, alpha males looking for their next prey, they moved on and all was well in the world. They did not care an inch for the pain they inflicted. All they cared about was the pain that had been alleviated with orgasmic nights under the sheets.

By the time he got back to work, Davey had determined the outcome of the night, and by the time he finished with work, he had convinced his scatter brain that this date was coming with no strings attached.

That didn't stop him, however, from going back on Cinderfella and reading Ave's profile once again. He needed solid proof.

Ave, 31

6ft, 154lbs

Greenwich Village, NY

About Me:

Barman, shopping aficionado, wine lover, cocktail master.

What I'm looking for:

Dunno. Meet people. Make friends. Go on dates. New in town, so someone to show me the secrets of NY.

It was all there. Where he said meet people, he

meant meet men, where he said make friends he meant make fuck-buddies. Where he said dates, he meant hookups, and where he said he was looking for someone to show him the secrets of the city, he meant the secrets of their bedroom. All the codes were there; Davey just hadn't taken the time to translate them.

A shower and a change of clothes later, he was ready for his "date" and with time to spare. That hardly ever happened. He decided to give his place a tidy-up. He would only see the guy for one night, but he didn't want him coming into a pigsty.

When he looked at his watch again, he realized he was now five minutes late.

Jeez

Thankfully they were only meeting a couple of blocks from his house, so he dashed out into the winter cold in a sweater, and ten minutes later he turned up to their designated meeting place, a small bar in the corner of the street, brought to life by social chatter and smokers. He finished his own cigarette and walked in. He had messaged Ave on Cinderfella about his lateness but wasn't sure if his message had been received, so he scanned the room, anxious to find him.

The place was warm from the fire emanating from the big fireplace in the middle of the room, and his bones immediately ached after running in the cold. The chatter created a constant buzz, and

Davey's ears were immediately molested by the hazard.

A gloved hand waved at him and on closer inspection he saw it belonged to Ave. He wore a burgundy sweater with matching gloves and white skinny jeans. His glasses were big and round and gave a clear view of his beautiful grey eyes that had a silver glint in the fire light. Wrapped around his neck was the pink and purple scarf he had purchased only yesterday.

He got no points for color coordination, but he was still more attractive than most people in there.

When he got to his table, Ave stood up and gave Davey a light hug. His beard was perfectly trimmed, and he smelled of alcohol and flowers, a perfume that matched his level of masculinity, which wasn't overbearing. He seemed to be a man comfortable in his body and in his sexuality.

Davey loved a man who knew who they were and their place in the world. It was something you only ever saw in older men. They'd been around, been through this or that shit and had a more realistic view of the world and their life.

Ave already had a glass of beer on the table, and as soon as Davey settled he got up to get him a drink as well. Davey couldn't resist looking at the man on his way to the bar. The buttocks under the jeans were firm and round. Just how Davey liked his men: With a good amount of ass on them.

He returned with two drinks, one for each, taking his seat back, he unwrapped the scarf and placed it with his coat on the chair behind him.

"Were you waiting long?" Davey apologized.

Ave took a sip and shook his head. "Literally got here two minutes before you did. I was lucky I found a table. This place is packed tonight," he said looking around.

"Yeah, it's why I fucking hate Christmas. Every kind of hopeless human goes out that one month and think they're kings or queens of the world," Davey commented, but Ave's look made him curse himself mentally.

He didn't want to come across as an asshole on the very first date.

And another mental slap reminded him this wasn't a date.

"Yeah, I have to agree. You get the weirdest people out during festive times. But I don't know. I quite like Christmas. If I wasn't so busy with work I think I'd enjoy it more," Ave said.

Davey pulled himself back. "My God! You *are* a weirdo!" he exclaimed and laughed. Thankfully, so did Ave.

"So…" Ave said dragging the word as long as he could and Davey knew what was coming. Are you top or bottom? What's your thing? Do you do safe sex? Have you been tested? Which one was it going to be? "I never actually asked your name. What is it?"

"Fuck!" Davey cursed. It was true. They weren't even on a first name basis. And his nickname on Cinderfella didn't count. DTop26 was not a name anyone could use publicly, and if they did, they didn't deserve his time of day. "I'm Davey. How did I never think to say? Or ask for that matter? Is yours Ave?"

Ave nodded. "Avery actually, but I thought not everyone needs to know my name. Not that it's hard to guess."

"Well, I didn't. But I'm stupid so I don't count," Davey said.

Avery frowned. "Oh, shut up. I'm sure you aren't."

It was nice of Avery to make an effort to be a decent human being before shacking up. It was even bordering on sweet.

"You haven't known me long enough, that's why you're saying that," he replied and drank half his beer in one gulp.

"Well, yeah, that's true, but tonight's a start, right?" Avery said, and when Davey cocked his head trying to understand what he'd just said, Avery rushed to add, "If we want it to be."

Maybe Davey had underestimated Avery and his intentions, but he could be misinterpreting what the man was saying. It wouldn't have been the first time. After all, what gay dude doesn't do sex on the first date? Or whatever this whole meeting was, anyway.

"Do you want to grab some food? I haven't eaten much today and I'm starving," Avery said.

Davey liked the sound of that. "Oh, yes please. I never say no to food. Do they do food here?" he asked. He couldn't bother walking in the cold again to find another place to eat.

"As a matter of fact, they do. They've got a restaurant on the back. Follow me," he said and stood up.

Davey followed him to the bar, where they swerved left and stood in front of a small counter where a lady was talking on the phone while scribbling something in a notebook in front of her. After two seconds she stopped writing, straightened her back and huffed.

"No, sir, we don't have space for sixty people in an hour. We don't take bookings this large last minute…" Davey assumed she had been interrupted, as she had not finished speaking. She listened on the other side of the phone, her hair frizzing the more they waited. "You're a troll. Bye, now," she said after a few more seconds and hung up.

Davey and Avery grimaced. The girl put her smile back on and greeted them.

"I'm sorry you had to witness that. Someone was

23

being an all-star douchebag on the phone," she explained and picked two menus in her hands. "Just the two of you?"

Davey nodded, and Avery placed his hand at the small of Davey's back giving him a light push. The tickle of his touch spread to his entire body. He licked his lips to prevent himself from moaning at the perfection.

"Don't worry about us. I work at a bar. I know what it's like," Avery said as the girl took them into the restaurant, another square room almost as big as the front bar and just as busy.

"Thanks. Well, allow me to not ruin your night any further. Take a seat, and I'll send a waitress over in a minute," she said and returned to her station.

"Dear God! I wasn't that hungry until all these smells hit my nose. I'm starving now," Davey said.

"Let's get you some food, then!" Avery responded and opened the menu, his eyes pinned on the man sitting opposite him.

His eyes looked emerald in the yellow-tinted room. Davey couldn't voice what it was, but something tugged inside him, something he had never felt before.

THREE

They handed the menus to their waitress, and Davey searched the room for details that would distract him from Avery's eyes that were so captivating. When he returned his gaze to the table, Avery was staring at his beer, stealing glances at Davey.

"Where do you work, Avery?" Davey couldn't stand the silence. Inquiring about his work was the first thing that came to his mind.

"I work downtown, at a cocktail bar close to Stonewall. You?" he said and then immediately laughed, apologizing for his awkwardness. "How long have you worked at John Logan?"

"Two years."

Avery nodded.

"You said you're new in town on your profile. How long have you been here for?" Davey asked.

Avery's eyes brightened at the question. "Only two months. I'm still settling in," he answered.

"Oh, so you are a newbie. Where did you come from?"

"I'm originally from Chatham, Massachusetts, but I moved to Seattle about a decade ago," Avery grabbed his glass and took a sip.

Their starters arrived and were placed in front of them. "Honey-glazed, goats cheese bread and olives and a strawberry and feta salad?" the waitress gave them a smile confirming she had the right food, and once she had she left them in peace.

"This looks lovely," Davey said looking at glistening bronze bread and cutting a small piece. He dipped it in the jar of olive oil and balsamic. "Seattle, huh? What took you all the way there?" he asked and ate the piece of bread only to be hit by a firework of flavors that forced him to close his eyes and enjoy.

When he opened them again, Avery was staring at him with a grin plastered on his face.

"I went to college there and kinda stuck around for a time after I finished it," he said and picked up an olive.

"What did you study?"

"Arts and psychology," he said with a nonchalance that made Davey want to slap him hard for making it sound as if it was nothing.

"You are an artist? And a psychologist? That's

incredible. I would love to see your work. Wait! It's not anything weird like nude incest live portraits or cow's blood paintings or anything, right? Because if it is, I'm good," he said, momentarily forgetting about the deliciousness of the food in front of him.

"Oh, good God. No. While very appealing ideas, indeed, I do nothing as fascinating. I just used to think I could paint. College proved to me that I can't. That's all," he said with the same indifference as before.

"So, you don't do art anymore? What about the psychology part?"

"I never actually liked the subject. It was just a compromise to get my parents off my back long enough to breathe," he said. "What did you study?"

"Nothing. Couldn't really afford it and I never really found my calling. I thought it would be illogical to get myself in debt for the rest of my life when I didn't even know what I would be doing the next day. When the recession hit, I was sure I'd made the right choice," he said. It wasn't a secret he struggled with money or that he didn't come from a rich family. Still admitting it to a complete stranger wasn't easy.

"Where are you from?" Avery asked as if he hadn't even heard Davey's previous statement. Or as if it hadn't bothered him.

"Madison, Wisconsin. But I moved out as soon as I was old enough to do so. I'm enough nuthouse on my own," he said. He wasn't even in control of his mouth anymore. His natural censor seemed to have abandoned him tonight while he was baring it all out for Avery.

Again, it was as if he hadn't heard him, because he laughed. "You look quite normal to me," he said and Davey squinted. "I mean, you don't look *or* sound crazy," he stuttered.

Was Avery nervous? Was the older, more sophisticated man afraid? Did he see it as a date? It certainly looked like it so far, since nothing related to bodily fluids had come up in conversation, but the night was still young and Davey was rarely wrong.

"What made you leave Seattle?"

Avery's smile that had formed during the short silence was scrubbed clean and he bit his cheek. "I never meant to stay there for the rest of my life. When I broke up with my boyfriend I knew it was high time I left the city."

"What happened?" Davey asked, but he realized how personal the question was so he added, "If you don't mind talking about it, of course."

Avery looked around them and shuffled his collar before continuing. "Let's just say we'd been together for too long, for all the wrong reasons."

"I see. I'm sorry," Davey said. He could tell Avery didn't like the subject.

"It's okay. What about you?

Davey paused and cocked his head to the side. "What about me?"

"How long have you been single?"

Davey didn't know how to answer the question. Honesty was always appreciated, granted that, but he didn't know how a date would take it if he told them he'd only been single a day. It would sound creepy. Weird. A little pathetic. And definitely not normal.

"A while. Never really been in a long-term relationship. I seem unable to keep 'em." As soon as he said it he wanted to punch himself, but it'd escaped his lips before he could control them.

"Entirely their fault, I'm sure," Avery smiled.

His smile was warm, it made him tingle. It was a comforting face. A face he could look into for hours. And those eyes. The candles lit on the tables gave them a twinkle that was to die for.

"So how is work? How are you finding the big city?" he asked Avery, unable to look away from him.

Avery grinned, stabbed a leaf of arugula, and chewed it delicately.

"It's different and all the same at the same time. Dunno. I like how busy it is and how more sophisticated people are, but at the same time I get a lot bigger personalities who act like the world is theirs for the taking," he said.

"Is that staff or customers?" Davey asked.

"Both," Avery laughed. "Staff that don't give a crap about their attitude, who can't smile for a nanosecond yet expect a generous tip, and then I get the customers that will demand a free round of cocktails because their fries took two minutes longer than they should have," Avery said and Davey found himself nodding.

"Or people who come up to you and say 'Oh, this has no tag. Is it free, then?' Like, go get some brains, human. How the fuck did they ever let you out?" he commented.

Avery laughed. It was a deep and gentle laugh, but genuine nonetheless.

"I have to admit something," he said but still looked hesitant.

Davey frowned. What kind of surprise did he have under his sleeve? Was he still in a relationship and had lied about the whole moving thing? Was it that he wasn't actually living in the city but was here on vacation? Or was it as simple as "You're a great person, but I don't think this is for me"? He had heard it all before. Seen it all. Experienced it all and so much more. He could take the blow.

"I lied about not working tonight. I was meant to work all day today, but I asked one of my managers to cover me so I could go out with you. I couldn't get you out of my head after I saw you at the store. And then when we started talking on the app… I'm glad I managed to get out of work and meet you," he said.

If Davey thought Avery was beautiful before, he was melting of swoon now. No one had ever told him anything as nice as that. Not even close. It made his body tingle with sensation and his stomach clench.

"That—that's very sweet. I don't know what to say," he said.

Avery smiled. "You can tell me what you do when you're not working at John Logan," he said and took a sip of his lager.

"Well, I like chugging beer, and I'm a master of binge watching," he chuckled.

Avery pursed his lips in a cheeky smile, and it made Davey's heart skip a beat. That was fucking cute. And damn hot!

"Any other excellent life skills?" He asked.

"Oh, yeah, I'm an excellent worrier. I can worry the crap out of a situation. Any situation. Just give me one," Davey went off without any hint of sarcasm in his tone, although Avery started chuckling, so that was a good sign.

"No need for that," he said, and the waitress stepped in as if on cue to pick up their starters and offer them another round of drinks, which they gladly took.

Davey looked to the other restaurant patrons and saw the blank, empty faces with the drowsy eyes fixed on phone screens, smart watches and tablets. Not an awful lot of people seemed to be engaging with their partners, but chatter was permeating in the room. You could tell who the couples on date were from the eyelashes flattering, the puckering lips, and the larger-than-life laughter that surrounded them.

"Do you have any family?" he finally asked Avery and Davey was happy to see him staring back at him.

"I do. My mom and dad live back in Chatham. With my little sister. My older sister is in Chicago living the life of a journalist," he said.

"What kind of journalism does she do?" Davey asked.

"Lifestyle, although she would love to do political one day. She's doing really well for herself," Avery said and there was a hint of a smile there that Davey didn't miss.

"So are you, though," he told him.

"Thank you," Avery replied as the waitress arrived with their new drinks and their food. A roast chicken dipped in red wine gravy and truffle oil mushrooms for Avery and lamb chops with pumpkin squash garnished with cider jus for Davey.

"What about your family?"

"What about my family?"

"Are they still living in Madison?" Avery said and tasted his chicken.

"My dad is. I don't really talk to him though," Davey admitted.

Avery paused and seemed unsure of his next question. "How come?"

Davey smudged his lips and blew raspberries. "It's what happens when your dad is an abusive little coward and your mom suffers the consequences for it," he said dismissively, trying to put as much apathy in his statement as possible.

It didn't work, judging by the sad look on Avery's face. Not that he minded. The guy looked cute in all his colors, and even though the current one was sympathy for his pain, Davey couldn't help but get turned on by his caring eyes.

"That's terrible. What about your mom? Where does she live?" Avery asked.

"In heaven," Davey said without missing a beat.

The color washed out of Avery's face and he put his fork down. "I'm so sorry, Davey. What happened?"

"Dad happened," Davey said simply.

Avery apologized again, but Davey didn't need it. It hadn't been Davey wo beat the crap out of his mom and sent her to the hospital with a concussion and internal bleeding. It was the monster in Madison who he was unfortunate enough to share his genes with.

"Any brothers or sisters?" Avery asked, the sadness lingering in his eyes. But now there was also something else there: interest. He was interested in Davey's story. He wasn't distracted by his phone or passing hunks. He wasn't checking the time on his watch. He was there for Davey. And he was drinking him up.

Davey's heart fluttered. Did it mean something? Was he supposed to memorize these feelings in case they made up a story for later in life? Or was it him going back to living in a fairy tale world with love at first sight and happy-ever-afters?

"No, no siblings. I'm an only child," he said.

"Okay," Avery responded, and he seemed stuck for words. Davey took him out of his misery and touched upon another subject.

"So..." he started but couldn't find a subject that would effectively take a burden off the solemn moment. "What do you think of the food?"

Avery nodded, chewing on his chicken and expressed his satisfaction. "It's lovely. That wine gravy is to die for. How is your lamb?"

Davey realized he hadn't tried his food yet, but he had been making patterns in his mash with his fork. "It's good," he said and dove into his dinner.

Both of them silently decided to consume their meal. It would have been uncomfortable, sitting with a stranger, unable to talk, chewing and biting in front of someone who didn't even know your favorite color. It should have been awkward. But it wasn't.

A lingering familiarity tugged at his shoulder and every few seconds he would look at Avery, who would return the stare with a smile.

What was going on here? He had been expecting a quick dinner and a brief encounter under the sheets, but he'd gotten more than he had hoped for. An intellectual talk. Someone who could hold a conversation. Someone who was interested in what he had to say.

All of a sudden he realized that it felt like he'd known Avery all his life. Sure, they didn't know anything about each other, but he was comfortable in Avery's presence. He was himself, sarcastic, apathetic and with his dry sense of humor, yet he wasn't judged, or ridiculed.

It took less time to finish their meals than he thought it would. When he put his napkin in the plate, he saw Avery do the same.

"That was so good," Davey said. "Excellent choice of restaurant. Can't believe I've never been in this place before. It's brilliant."

"I'm glad you liked it. Desserts?" He bit his lip in a naughty smile that made Davey hungry, but not for food.

"Only if you share it with me. I'm bloated," he answered and the smile became a laughter.

Davey's eyes glistened again.

He could get used to this. Get used to looking into those eyes and getting drunk in their sincerity.

He could get used to looking at the cheeky smile, lips pursed and wet, begging to be kissed.

Dinner finished on a high note with a sauté of bananas drizzled with maple syrup and cardamom flowers on an oat pancake. Avery asked for the check, and when the waitress brought it over, he placed his card on the table. Even though Davey protested, he paid the check in full.

As they exited the restaurant area and returned to the busy and loud bar side, Avery put his hand on Davey's arm and bent closer. Was he going to kiss him? Did he literally find this moment to do it out of all of them? When they were on the move and in a noisy bar?

Avery shouted in his ear and Davey was washed with relief. "Do you want to walk?"

Davey shrugged. "I don't mind," he replied, and Avery led the way outside.

The weather had gotten worse since he'd come in the bar, and he had no jacket. Just his thick woolen sweater to protect him from the chilly wind that had gone up in the streets.

They walked the opposite direction to his house, and it had been an intentional action by Davey. He had prepared for the end of dinner all day, making sure he was trimmed and clean and smelled nice, but after such a great date, he didn't want to jump into bed with Avery. Not that he didn't find the man attractive. In fact, he found him irresistible. But having sex with him now would make him feel as if there was nothing different to their date than any other date or booty call. T

he animalistic need taking over and all feelings and emotions be damned. He had slept with many a guy on the first date and they never seemed to work out. He didn't want the same to happen with Avery. He was too damn cute to be a fling.

They walked a couple blocks and Davey was shaking. The cold had sunk through to his bones and his teeth ground against each other. He didn't know what he'd been thinking when he went out. It was still December; the weather was getting worse by the day. He should have known better.

"Are you okay?" Avery asked him.

Davey nodded but it didn't convince Avery.

"Are you cold?" Another nod from Davey, and Avery stopped him by gripping both his shoulders. "Here, take my coat. I'm okay," he said and unzipped his jacket.

Davey shook his head. "No, it's fine. I'll be okay. Don't worry." He continued walking.

Avery didn't follow him. "Davey, you are putting on my coat and I'm not hearing another word," he raised his voice and made Davey turn to stone.

Had he just ordered him to do something? He turned around and saw Avery holding the jacket in both hands and waiting for Davey to slip into it. Okay, that was hot. He let himself follow Avery's orders. When he turned to face him again, Avery gripped the zipper and pulled it all the way up.

His hands lingered on the base of Davey's neck for a moment, and Davey took Avery in. That smile was infecting his face again. The pursed lips, the puppy eyes. Davey couldn't resist them any longer. He pushed closer and locked his lips with Avery's. An explosion of emotions burst inside of him, and his cock stirred up without much provocation.

His lips looked small, but upon kissing them, Davey fought the urge to bite the lower lip with hunger. Instead he slipped his tongue between Davey's lips and asked for permission by licking them.

Avery reciprocated by opening his mouth and putting his own tongue in action. There was tenderness in the kiss. When Avery's hands cupped his face, it turned to magic. The warmth of his hands made Davey breathless.

That, right there, was perfection. He immediately wished he could freeze time in that moment and savor it forever.

Avery pulled away, slowly but painstakingly nonetheless, and he felt the absence straight away.

This was torture. Kissing those lips and then being deprived of them was one of the cruelest things someone could inflict on him.

"Do you want to grab one last drink?" Avery asked, and Davey smiled.

He took Davey across the street and down another block where they found a rustic bar called The Craft with a wide selection of ales from around the world. It had no space indoors. It was a small space, and the glass panel door had been slid open to allow access to the bar that stretched from one end of the shop to the other. Avery ordered two beers, and they stood by a table watching the passing traffic.

Davey was still cold. He sipped his beer, hoping it would warm him up, but it didn't have such an effect. Avery took Davey's beer, put it down and slid his arms around him. Davey buried his face in Avery's sweater, which was as soft as his touch and he listened to Avery's heartbeat. It had a quick erratic pace, and Davey tried to synchronize the tempo with his own heartbeat. It took him a few minutes to realize that would never happen.

They spent a lot of time in that position, only removing themselves from each other to have some of their drinks but returned to the embrace immediately after.

"Right," Avery said, and Davey felt Avery's chest tremble with the rumbling of his voice. Davey pulled back. Avery was looking at his watch. "I think I need to go. It's getting late, and I've got an early start tomorrow. Can I walk you home?"

Davey had to take a moment to get used to conversation again. He rubbed his eyes and yawned as if he had just woken up, but all he had done was sober up from the proximity of Avery's body to his.

"It's okay. You don't have to. Let me walk you to the subway," he said, and they left the bar walking side by side.

Avery brushed his fingers across Davey's and took his hand. The walk was very short, and Davey stood at the top of the stairs before seeing Avery off.

"I had an amazing time," he said.

"We should do this again," Avery agreed.

Davey smiled. "You want to?"

"Of course," Avery exclaimed. "You're the sanest person I've met in the city in all this time. I could get used to your company."

Davey looked away. This was way too much. He certainly was dreaming. There was no way any of this was real.

"Me too," he agreed. "Before I forget," he continued and unzipped the jacket to hand it back to Avery.

"No, keep it. I wouldn't want you to catch your death on your way back," Avery said, pulling back.

Davey refused to accept that. "I'm only three blocks away. I'll survive. Take your jacket back," he said.

Avery insisted.

"Avery, I won't take your jacket with me. If you refuse to take it, I will simply leave it here," he said and put it on the subway railing. "I'm sure a homeless person will appreciate it."

Avery laughed. "Okay. But you have to take my scarf. It's big and warm. It should keep you safe on your way back."

Davey shook his head, but Avery was already putting it around his neck.

"Please! Besides, now you have to meet with me again to give it back," he said and poked Davey's stomach with his finger.

Davey laughed. "Okay."

Avery put his hand on the back of Davey's head and planted another passionate kiss on him. Then he proceeded down the stairs, leaving Davey flustered and horny. This man was something else.

FOUR

When he got in, his phone was already ringing with new messages from Avery. These ones were on his actual phone and not on Cinderfella.

He closed the door to his apartment and kicked his shoes across the room. He didn't take the scarf off. It still smelled of Avery. It smelled of security and comfort. He wished he would never have to take it off. But he had to give it back, and that meant he had to meet Avery again, and being in his presence far outweighed being in the presence of his articles of clothing.

Hey, you! Thanks for the most beautiful evening I've ever had, read the message from Avery.

An infectious smile crept up on him as he read the message, his fingers hovering over the buttons before he knew to control them. *I had the best time, also. Hope to see you again soon.*

The reply came in a nanosecond. *When?*

Davey laughed.

This guy!

He settled on his couch and turned the TV on. He flipped to a music channel before he turned his attention back to his cell. He was off work tomorrow and doing a double the following day. He really wanted to ask Avery out for tomorrow, but he was afraid it would be too soon, that it would scare the guy away.

To hell with it. If it scared him away, Davey didn't need to bother.

I'm free tomorrow, he said.

He watched as a pop rendition of "Jingle Bells" displayed on the screen when his phone popped.

I'm working all day, but I'll ask around for cover. I'll get back to you on that one.

Okay, Davey replied simply.

Can't wait to see you again, Avery said.

Me neither, Davey texted.

He assumed the conversation was over until Avery knew if he could make it tomorrow. It wasn't.

I miss you.

The message hit him with surprise. It wasn't often guys wore their hearts on their sleeve and displayed their emotions so blatantly, so quick.

Was he being more sexual than Davey had

determined he was? Or was he simply taking a leap of faith and hoping it took off?

He didn't know how to reply. The more he thought of Avery, however, the more he realized the statement held true for him too. He'd only known the guy for three hours, and he couldn't get Avery's cute smile and beautiful eyes off his mind. It was strange. A peculiar feeling that he could get used to.

I miss you too. Wish you were here with me so I could look into your eyes again.

Avery responded immediately. *:) you are amazing.*

I know :P, he replied.

And cocky from the looks of it, Avery said.

If only you knew how much :P

The TV played endless Christmas tunes, and Davey was so engulfed in the chat that the sound irritated him.

"Fucking Christmas!" he said as he switched the set off and was surrounded by silence again. Silence, but not solitude. Avery was still on the other side of the phone texting something.

Would you be okay if we Skyped? I can't sleep yet and I want to see your face before I go to bed, it said.

Davey didn't know how he felt about Skyping. He'd done naughty things on Skype. *Only if you keep your hands where I can see them,* he responded.

Hahaha, was the reply and immediately after his phone started ringing.

Davey answered the call and he was greeted by

Avery's face all snuggled in his comforter, lying on his bed. Davey smiled.

"Hey, beautiful," he said.

"Hey," Davey replied.

God it felt good being in his presence again, virtual as it was. It made the living room brighter. What on earth was happening to him?

"Whatchu doing?" he asked.

Avery pushed the comforter away and he was illuminated by his bedside table lamp. "Just resting. The house is a bit cold so I've thrown myself under the comforter until the heating takes effect. You?"

Davey looked around him. There was nothing around. Nothing of interest. "Nothing. Was listening to some music, but it was too Christmasy and got bored. What time are you working tomorrow?"

"Eleven. Got to pick up some stuff beforehand, though, so I've got an early start. Again," he said.

Davey rolled his eyes. "Don't say anymore. Eleven is early enough for me," he laughed. "So, what are you picking up?"

Avery looked away from the camera and Davey was worried he had asked a personal question unknowingly. "My ex sent me a couple of boxes that I left behind, so I'm picking them up from the post office," he replied.

"Oh," was all Davey managed to say.

"Oh, indeed," he repeated with grin. "Do you

want to sleep? Should I hang up?" he asked innocently.

Davey couldn't imagine anything worse at that moment. Being separated from Avery a second time in the same day. That was surely what nightmares were made of.

He shook his head. Avery smiled.

"Not just yet," he said.

"Okay. What are your plans for tomorrow?"

Davey hadn't had the chance to make any plans. He could always take Avery to his favorite restaurants, maybe go clubbing, although that carried a lot of dangers with a new date. He needed time to think. "Not sure yet. What did you want to do?"

"Anything," Avery replied. "But I meant what are your plans for the day while you're off?"

Davey rolled his eyes at himself. "God, I'm such an idiot," he said.

"You are not," Avery was quick to comment.

"Trust me. You don't know me well enough," he insisted.

"I'm hoping you'll give me a chance to do so," he said.

Davey smiled. Why did he know to say all the right things?

"Doing anything tomorrow, then?"

"Not sure yet, actually. I wanted to go shopping for clothes, and meet up with a couple of friends, but they haven't got back to me yet, so I might just stay home and make some stuff."

"What kind of stuff?" Avery asked with a hint of innuendo.

Davey looked around his flat at all of his creations and felt a twang of embarrassment. Avery was an arts graduate; he could create real art, nothing like what Davey made. It was hardly art. It was hardly anything. It was all worthless. He still enjoyed making them. So maybe they *were* worth something.

"Like picture frames," he finally said before he could change his mind.

He looked on to his screen and waited for Avery's response.

"Picture frames?" he asked.

Davey almost burst out laughing. "Yeah, I make picture frames from scratch," he said.

Without missing a beat, Avery replied, "That's quite... an unusual hobby." Davey nodded, dropping his head in front of him. "I would love to see them one day. You've piqued my interest, mister," he added.

Davey sighed with relief and looked into the screen, meeting Avery's eyes, and even though a whole screen, and distance separated them, even though they weren't actually looking at each other but into an empty camera, it felt like they were looking at each other's soul.

"I think I'm gonna go to bed now," Avery said.

"I thought you already were," Davey teased him.

Avery laughed. "You know what I mean. My eyes are feelings heavy. I better leave you to it. Wouldn't wanna keep you up."

"You're not. But I'll let you go. I can see you're exhausted." The truth was he felt drained as well. He had been working the whole day and then went straight to the date. It was now a little past one, and his brain needed a rest. His splitting headache was proof enough. "Good night, handsome."

"Good night," Avery said, and they hung up.

The room felt empty again, but instead of sulking, he decided to get to bed and stop his mind from wandering, overthinking things. He brushed his teeth and went out like a light.

The next morning, he woke up refreshed. He'd had a dreamless sleep but felt more rested than he had in days. When he turned to read the time on his phone, he realized it was nine. It was only nine, and he had woken up without the help of an alarm. His friends had still not responded, so he decided to stay home until midday and then do some shopping. After all, he had a new man to impress and he desperately needed a new wardrobe.

He brewed some coffee and set his mug on his workstation. There was a neat box with all his tools organized accordingly. He grabbed a felt board and cut its shape into that of a heart. He didn't know why he'd chosen that shape. He usually made rectangles or squares. Hearts were cheesy.

He then took copper wire out of the wire box and started weaving it around the frame in haystack shapes, dropping a few beads in between. That took him a long time to finish.

He didn't like having asymmetry in his creations and it showed in his display. He looked over at the various picture frames standing on a shelf or hanging on the wall above and below it, all empty of pictures, but all without a hint of imperfection.

When he finished, he had a heart frame with warm, copper colors encasing it. He left it to dry and got off his station.

He looked at the time, and he was still ahead of schedule. He had another coffee, then got dressed and set off for Times Square.

His friends were assholes. No one had bothered replying to him or calling him, so he decided not to bother either. He would do the spree on his own. He was nothing if not used to his own company anyway.

He started going on the lookout for pants since he only owned one good pair and everything else had faded, worn off or shrunk with time and he hadn't had the funds or time, or willingness to replace them until now.

As he was coming out of the first store, his phone bleeped in his pocket and he withdrew it.

There was a message from Avery. It made his breath hitch, and he forgot where he was headed for a moment.

Hey, I managed to get tonight off. Hope you can still make it, handsome. Let me know x, read the message.

He was used to the men in his life not having the time of day for him unless it was for sex or clubbing. He was used to the men in his life finding excuses or simply being too lazy to arrange to see him. He was used to being a third wheel in a relationship, coming right behind everyone's jobs, ambitions, and personal life.

And there was Avery. He'd only known him for two days; he'd only seen him a handful of hours, hardly knew anything about him, and he had already made two arrangements to see him, changing his schedule so that he could spend time with him.

Davey hadn't known such a breed of man existed. But he wasn't going to overthink it. For all he knew Avery still wanted just sex. Maybe he liked to become friends with his fuck buddies. Maybe he was just a friendly, nice guy. Even thinking that of Avery, he didn't feel right. The man was different; he just needed to accept it.

"Thanks for taking the entire pavement, asshole," shouted a passerby in a suit as he ran past Davey, shaking him off his inner thoughts.

Right. He needed tops and he needed tops now,

and nice ones too, to impress Avery, he told himself, and he continued his spree with a spring in his step.

———

THEY SAT ON THE CHAISE-LOUNGE AND WARMED themselves up with a mug of mulled wine. The fire pit in front of them kept their feet and legs warm. It was a good thing, as Davey's new shoes were so thin he had been certain he was going to lose his toes to frostbite.

They were seated in The High Line. It had been turned into a small Winter Wonderland, with Christmas trees lined up across the old rail tracks and lit by colorful fairy lights, fake snow banks for children and adults to play in. There was also a mini skating rink, and beyond that, a bar with dozens of chairs and small fire pits to keep everyone warm.

Avery and Davey had been standing around for twenty minutes before they were able to grab a seat together in relative privacy, but it had been worth it, since they were now snuggled up in a large chair that just about fit both of them.

Avery was wearing his scarf again, but Davey assumed he hadn't thought he would get it back today, as the rest of his wardrobe was a completely different color scheme. He wore black jeans and a brown sweater with a green beanie. Avery's glasses were slightly frosted when he turned to look at Davey, and Davey's insides ached.

Avery was a sight to behold. And yet he was choosing to spend his time with a weirdo like Davey.

"Like the shoes," Avery said, looking at his crossed legs, and Davey looked at his own as well.

"Thanks," he said. "They are really thin, though, so I'm fuh-reezing!"

Avery sat up. "Are you sure you want to stay out here then? I don't mind going someplace else," he said.

"It's okay," Davey shook his head. "I'm not made of paper. I'll survive. Besides, the fire is keeping me warm," he said.

Avery sat back down on the chair and grinned. "Thank God! 'Cause I really like it here."

Davey agreed.

Certainly, the Christmas enthusiasm that was overflowing around him was not the best—he could do without the screaming children and the sickening kissing couples wearing Santa hats and the college students going crazy on the ring—but he was by a fire with Avery, and that made everything better.

"What did you end up doing today?" Avery started, and Davey told him all about his day. Avery did the same, with much less interest. Instead he turned the subject to Davey yet again and his unusual hobby.

"I like making things with my own hands. You can control the quality of the product, and it gives me great satisfaction when I finish."

He sighed at the double entendre he had just made, hoping that Avery hadn't noticed, although the smirk on the man's face said otherwise.

"It's also very therapeutic. When my mom passed away, it's the one thing that kept me sane. It kept my mind off the horror, the loneliness, the anger, and grief and focused it on making something new," he said, the memory of that time in his life bringing sorrowful tingles around his eyes and nose.

Avery didn't comment on the misery. He nodded and pursed his lips in understanding. "Why picture frames?"

Davey shuffled in his seat, but answering the question was unavoidable. He could lie. But he couldn't bring himself to look at Avery's eyes and spout anything but truth.

"Because they are keepers of memories," he simply said, and he could already see Avery's eyes squinting in confusion. He was ready for the question that followed, and he answered it. "They hold pictures, memories of another time, a happy time. They can hold your entire life's happiest moments in a few snapshots. I just make the package look pretty. The rest is up to the person to fill in," he said.

"So do you sell them?" Avery asked, and his

question was justified. Davey shook his head. "I see," Avery commented. "I would love to see your collection of memories one day."

Davey was also ready for that. A lot of his past relationships and dates had asked the same thing, after getting over the initial weirdness of his hobby. It was usually at this point where Davey faltered, as he knew how the next answer sounded to a stranger.

"I don't have any, actually."

Confusion crossed Avery's face again. "What do you mean?"

"I mean, I don't have any memories. Okay, that's a lie. I have a few pictures from when I traveled, but otherwise my frames are empty," he explained.

Avery cocked his head to the side, not understanding.

"How is that possible? Are you not a picture person, or…?" he started, but Davey cut him off.

"My father threw out all of my pictures."

"What?"

Davey continued. "When my mother died, in the hospital, after he pushed her down the stairs and she got a concussion, he went crazy. He thought his wife abandoned him, that she chose to leave him rather than live *with* him, so he threw out all of her pictures. When I blamed him for her death, he threw away my stuff, pictures included, saying he didn't have a family anymore; he didn't need to see their faces when everyone deserted him. So I've got no pictures from my high school graduation or the day I was born, from prom, from my graduation, and I have no pictures of my mom. She's just in here," he said and pointed to his head.

Avery's eyes were red and shone with tears. He didn't say anything. He just kissed Davey. It was not an erotic kiss. It was comfort. It was compassion. It was care.

Click!

He turned and saw Avery holding his phone, having snapped a picture of them. He turned his phone around and looked at it, then showed it to Davey.

"What is this?" he asked. It was them, kissing. Lights were a blur behind them and it was very low-light, but it was pretty.

"It's the start of new memories. With me," he said.

Davey stared at him.

"If you want to," he added.

Davey smiled. "Yes, I do."

Avery kissed him again.

FIVE

Davey kissed Avery with passion. He had missed the lips, the eyes, the man. It had been a long day at work. Jimmy had been on him all day, constantly asking him questions and challenging his work. Customers had been snotty bastards, rude and way too engaged in their own lives to pay any attention to him while he was helping them out.

Seeing Avery after a long day of work was his immediate caffeine fix. He could hardly remember what he ever did after work before Avery came into his life, and he'd only been dating him for a week.

"Where to, baby?" Avery asked him and hung on to Davey's mouth until he answered.

"Let's go to Sally's. We had a great time last time, didn't we?" he said and Avery agreed.

"Well you did. I was too busy staring down everyone who flirted with you," he commented, and Davey laughed.

"I think they were flirting with you, but — let's agree to disagree on that. You've got nothing to worry about. I've only got eyes for you," he said, and Avery gave him his signature smile.

Avery pulled his hand and waited for a cab to stop. As soon as they found one, they jumped in and warmed up to the heater until it was time to get out again and brave the winter cold. The entire street was illuminated by fairy lights and Christmas decorations, and the few trees that aligned on the pavement were dressed with fake snow and mistletoes.

Avery took Davey's hand and entered the bar, which was starting to get crowded. Avery headed for the bar, but Davey pulled him back. Avery voiced his objection, but only until Davey kissed him to shut him up. A gentle, soft kiss that made him warmer in the groin area than he dared to admit.

He wanted Avery with all his being. He couldn't get the man out of his head. He wanted to give him all he had and then some, but so far, the idea of sleeping together hadn't even been a subject of their conversations.

Not that they didn't both want it. Davey could

tell that Avery wanted him as much as he did. The unmistakable horny eyes and flushed skin made up for the words they didn't think appropriate to speak.

But the fact that they hadn't jumped to bed had only worked to cement Davey's belief that Avery was more than a fuck. He was an entirely different thing altogether. Davey was still trying to piece out what it was he was after. No one would have wasted almost ten days on someone just for a quickie and a rapid escape. Avery wanted more than that. Davey could tell by the way he answered the phone every time Davey called him, and he could tell by the way Avery referred to him when messaging him.

Davey pulled away from Avery and they both looked above them at the mistletoe. Avery laughed.

"You're so romantic," he said.

Davey smiled. "And you're a good kisser. So, it's got nothing to do with romance," he told him.

"But I like romance," Avery whined, pouting.

Davey's heart skipped. "I like it, too," he whispered and gave Avery another peck before they proceeded into the bar and took a seat by the window.

The place was full of gay men, although it wasn't advertised as a gay bar. A lot of muscled and trimmed men worked behind the bar, and burly, older guys worked the security at the door. The table tops were decorated with Christmas cards and miniature trees as well as red candle holders.

At first they sat opposite each other, but even at that short distance, Davey suffered from withdrawal, so Avery moved his chair next to Davey's. They sipped their mulled wine and talked about work until Avery caught the gaze of a guy.

"Is he looking at you? Is he fucking stupid? He can see me sitting next to you, holding your hand, yet he's still flirting with you. Argh...men," he said.

Davey laughed and placed his palm on Avery's face. "Like I said, only eyes for you, my baby," he said.

Avery smiled. "I know. It's not you." He waved around Davey. "It's them I'm worried about. They won't keep off. I mean I understand where they're coming from. Who could resist such a handsome man? But you're mine," he said with a childish pout that Davey couldn't help loving.

"You're adorable. You know?" Davey grinned as Avery turned to look at him. "And I am glad to be yours."

Avery ducked and kissed him on the lips, lingering as if he couldn't decide whether he wanted to pull away or stay there forever.

When Davey started talking, he didn't have a choice. Despite loving the contact, Davey felt uncomfortable staying connected for so long in public.

"My father called me today," Davey said.

Avery frowned and sat back in his chair. "What did he want?"

Davey shrugged. "No clue. I didn't pick up. He probably butt-dialed me," he said trying to insert as much nonchalance as possible.

Avery saw right through it. "Why don't you call him and see what he wanted? It could be something serious," he said.

"I have nothing to say to the man. I don't care if he lives or dies. He's already dead to me," Davey said, and he hoped his words carried as little care as he could.

"Still. You don't know what it was. Maybe you should try talking to him," Avery explained.

Davey shrugged. "Yeah, we'll see."

"It's so funny you got a call from your dad on the same day I had a missed called from my ex," he said.

Worry took over Davey and filled him to the brim with it. "What?" he tried to sound casual, but he couldn't. Lately, he was wearing his feelings on his sleeve when it came to Avery.

"Yeah, I don't know what he wanted. He was probably calling to ask if I got the boxes okay. Nothing to worry about." He comforted Davey and wrapped his arms around him, planting a kiss on his cheek.

"I do have a confession, though," he whispered in his ear.

"What is that?" Davey said with a worrying frown.

"I absolutely hate it here," he said.

Davey stared at him, waiting for the real confession, but it never came. "Is that all?" Avery nodded. "Why didn't you say so?"

"Well, you liked it here, and I didn't want to disappoint you, but I don't like it here," he said.

"Why?"

"Because I hate the way everyone is looking at you, like you are sexual prize, and everyone trying to get your attention by staring at you like there's no tomorrow," he explained.

Davey was stunned by his words. He couldn't believe Avery felt so possessive of him in such a short amount of time.

And it wasn't an aggressive possessiveness. It was an insecure one, which made it all the sweeter. It made Davey like Avery more. It made him want to kiss him.

And he did.

"You're the cutest," he told Avery.

Avery stood up and held his hand out for him. "Come on, let's go," he said.

"Where?"

Avery hesitated but didn't stop. "My home. If you want," he said.

Davey almost jumped out of the window in his rush to get out of the bar with Avery, and they hopped into a cab as soon as they hit the streets. It was a short ride to the Village, and when they got out at a side street, Avery dragged Davey up the stairs of an old building.

When he opened the door on the second floor, he was greeted with a cozy bachelor's apartment. It consisted of an open plan kitchen and living room, garnished with pants and shirts everywhere. A door led to the bathroom, and the one next to it to the bedroom.

"Excuse the mess," Avery said.

Davey didn't mind at all. The place had brick-lined warehouse walls and large windows that gave a view of the busy avenue outside. He took a seat on the couch and Avery brought beer for the both of them. Avery sipped a little and then lay back on the couch.

"Ah, finally some privacy. And no gawking eyes nosing in on our business," he said.

Some privacy indeed.

Davey saw that as a welcome change to the constant dates in public places where they had to restrict themselves to decent levels of intimacy. Not that he hadn't enjoyed spending time getting to know Avery.

He knew his favorite color and favorite food by now, as well as his birthday and full name. There was only one thing he didn't know that seemed it was going to be an issue in the immediate future.

"Do you want to watch something?" Avery asked.

Avery was so close to him. Davey could smell the fabric softener on Avery's clothes and smell his beer breath. He wanted nothing more than to take this man and show him how he felt. Davey leaned forward, not answering the question but going for Avery's wet lips.

Avery was hesitant. He kissed softly at first with his lips brushing Davey's sweetly. It was Davey who deepened the kiss but not before Avery got more comfortable. He put both hands on the man's head and mounted him, sitting on his lap with his hard-on stretching his new pants and Avery's throbbing cock under him.

Their tongues connected, wetting each other and licking with all the passion that had been brewing for over a week. Avery rubbed his hands on Davey's lower waist, and Davey's boner intensified at the suggestive touch.

Davey placed his own hands at Avery's neck and slid them down to his chest, which was built and strong. He moaned into Avery's mouth, and Avery took in a deep breath.

Their lips never parted, remaining stuck together in an indefinite kiss. Davey pushed his pelvis closer to Avery, and he could feel the man's erection throb under his balls. He grabbed Avery's hands, which had settled on Davey's waist, and guided them to his butt cheeks, where Avery squeezed and massaged them. Davey was so close.

He slowly got off Avery and unzipped his pants. Avery ruffled Davey's hair while Davey uncovered the penis hiding under the underwear and took all of it in in one hungry go. Avery moaned loudly, his pleasure echoing across the apartment. Davey began the smooth motions, stroking the dick with his mouth and using his fingers to double the effort, sending Avery into a delirium.

Avery pulled on Davey's hair the more he sucked him, and Davey's own erection ached in his trousers. Avery brought him back onto the couch and pulled his pants down. Davey felt Avery's hands as they unhooked the buttons, and the wetness soaking his boxers told him it wouldn't be long before the precum on his crotch would turn into a full load.

Avery took hold of his dick and, with a thirsty look, nipped on the head, staring at Davey as he was driven to a slow and painfully satisfying orgasm.

Avery's hands went searching under Davey's sweater and found his nipples, which he played with as he continued the blowjob hands-free.

Davey placed his hands on top of Avery's head and pushed him farther down, making him swallow Davey's cock all the way to the root.

Avery did with no resistance, and once he was in

for good, moaned, the vibrations of the man's vocal chords reverberating through Davey's entire body and sending him closer to the edge.

When his dick pulsed and he felt the release of his cum, his limbs loosened, and Avery came up to him for a kiss. His eyes radiated need. The need for him. Davey just hoped Avery could see the same need in his eyes. Since he wasn't sure, he searched for Avery's cock and stroked it until Avery's eyes shut, his mouth opened wide and his face morphed into something beautiful as he came on top of Davey's stomach.

Avery sighed.

Davey pulled him down and let their bodies rub against each other, hugging him as tight as his muscles would allow him. Avery sighed again, and his breath warmed Davey's heart.

They fell asleep in each other's arms.

———

HE WOKE UP THE NEXT MORNING IN A TANGLE OF arms and legs, and it took him a few good seconds to figure out which were his and which belonged to the body next to him.

Avery was still asleep, the rays of the sun caressing his peaceful face. Davey rubbed his cheek, and he saw the man's lips twitch, but his eyes remained closed. Then he turned his back on

Davey, giving him the cue he needed to get out of bed.

He tiptoed to the kitchen, the cold of the hardwood floor penetrating his skin and giving him the chills until he reached the carpeted kitchen. He massaged the back of his hands, creating friction and warmth in his arms, yet the rest of him was still subject to the cruel dampness of the apartment.

He opened the fridge and found a few microwaveable meals, soft drinks and beers, and a few necessities such as butter, milk, and cheese.

Next he opened the cupboards looking for the one thing he needed before anything else. He found some granules of coffee and some sugar and scraped up a watery mug before he collected the ingredients and tools he needed to make breakfast.

Ten minutes had passed, and as he was plating the food, Avery crossed the space between the bedroom and the kitchen with a stifled yawn and sat on one of the stools.

"What's all this?" he asked.

"It's a magical substance called breakfast. It tends to give nourishment in the mornings before battles," Davey sang and sipped from his coffee.

"You shouldn't have," Avery replied.

"Well, I did," Davey responded and came next to Avery. "Good morning," he said and kissed the man on the lips.

Avery returned the tender kiss and mumbled a greeting as well.

"Coffee?" Davey asked. "Although you seem to be running out. I can pop out to get some."

Avery frowned. "Hey, you're the guest. I'm the host, mister. I should be pampering you," he said, but Davey called nonsense. "Besides, there's coffee in the spares cupboard," he finished.

Davey stared at Avery with a questioning look and Avery got off the chair and opened a cupboard under the kitchen island. There were boxes of different non-perishables there, including coffee.

"What is all this?" he asked Avery.

Avery paused a beat. "It's time to find out about my quirks."

Davey took a deep breath. "All right. I think I'm ready. Shoot!"

"It's the spares cupboard. I don't like piling too much of the same thing in the other cupboards, but also don't like running out for every little thing every two seconds, so I buy in bulk and hide them all in here until it's time to refill," he said as if it was the most natural thing in the world.

"My God, you're incredible," Davey said simply.

"So are you," Avery replied.

They stared at each other smiling. After a few awkward seconds, Davey grabbed a jar of coffee and set off to make Avery a cup.

"I had a great time last night," Avery said.

Davey replied and poured the hot water in the mug. "I did too. We should repeat it another time."

Avery responded with a blush to Davey's naughty grin. "Any time," he answered.

"So—I've been meaning to ask you. If it's not too forward... if it is, just tell me, no hard feelings —" Davey started as he stirred the instant coffee.

"What is it?" Avery asked.

"Sugar? Milk?" he asked. Avery nodded for both and Davey passed him his coffee. "I'm having a great time with you, and I don't know if it's too soon or something," he started.

"Just come out with it, babe," Avery said.

"Do you have any plans for Christmas? Would you like to spend it with me?" Davey said and took a seat opposite Avery.

Avery set his coffee back down on the table and licked his lips. "I would love to spend Christmas with you. Why would that be too soon?"

Davey shrugged. "Dunno. I don't know if we're dating or just getting to know each other. I don't want to send you running for the hills by being too forward."

"The only reason why I would run for the hills would be to come after you. I like you, Davey. You're a beautiful man, inside and out. I can't believe my luck to have found you. And if you feel the same way, I'd like to keep you for as long as possible," Avery said. Davey blushed again. "Sorry, that came out wrong," he said looking for Davey's eyes.

"No." Davey met his eyes and looked into them. The sparkle, the life in them made him giddy with desire and... could it be love? So soon? "It came out just right."

SIX

They met on Monday a couple days later and went on a shopping binge for Christmas Day supplies.

They headed to Little Italy and browsed several shops before actually stopping in one. It was full of tacky, old holiday decorations and some beautiful trees.

Davey couldn't remember the last time he'd celebrated the holidays. He couldn't remember the last time he'd celebrated with someone he cared about.

Or he did, but he preferred not to think about it. It was exactly seven years ago, when his mom and dad had a wonderful family dinner cooked by none other than his mom. They'd exchanged gifts and she had bought him the computer he'd been begging for the past year. And even though it was expensive, she'd saved money and got it for him. His dad hadn't liked the price tag that came with the motherly sentiment.

A few days later, she was dead, and Davey had to return the computer so that he could afford a decent funeral for her. The thoughts made his eyes shine, and he wiped at them with his sleeve.

Avery was looking at waist-height trees, touching their needles and assessing thickness and softness, while Davey's eyes fell on a silvery white tree. He walked toward it and admired its difference. It stood out. It was different. It was made of fiber-optic and PVC. It was beautiful.

"What about this one?" he asked, and Avery joined him in a couple of strides. He placed his hand on Davey's lower back and inspected the tree that Davey had found.

"It's not bad. I like it," he said.

"Really?"

"No, but I can see you like it and that's more important," Avery said.

Davey rolled his eyes. "Then let's find something we both like." He rolled onto the next tree, a fluorescent green and blue that didn't remind him at all of holidays. When he turned around to see where Avery was, he was carrying the white tree under one arm, smiling with nonchalance and heading towards the counter. Davey chased after him.

"What are you doing?" he asked Avery.

71

"Everything else looks crap. This tree stands out, so it's a winner," he replied and set the tree on the counter.

"So... we're not going to decorate it? Just dump it in the middle of the room?" Davey teased and poked Avery's waist with his finger.

Avery looked at Davey and shook his head. "Can you hold that here?" he asked the cashier.

The lady, an aged woman dressed in a cotton T-shirt and an antler hat, nodded, and they ventured back to the main corridors of the store.

Shopping with someone made the experience not feel half as bad as he would have found doing it on his own. Selecting Christmas balls and bows while everyone around appeared as excited as if they'd done two joints and some E, he found the experience daunting at best. How could all these people keep calm and happy when they were surrounded by dozens, hundreds even, of their like? Davey shuddered but washed the feelings off his brain as he marched side by side with Avery.

Avery took his hand in his and squeezed it. It was reassuring and warm, just like the eyes that burned his insides every time they looked at him and the kisses that made him feel wanted. Avery peered at Davey and then stood in front of him, putting his arms around Davey's waist and bending down for a kiss.

"What are you thinking about?" he asked when he retrieved himself from Davey.

"You," he answered.

"But I'm here," Avery squinted.

"Indeed you are," Davey said and planted a kiss on his lips before he went browsing at all the tree decorations on display. "These are nice," he said and picked up a box of black diamonds and balls with silver glitter patterns drawn on them.

"Well, aren't you a little morbid, Wednesday Addams?" Avery chuckled.

"We have a white tree," he retorted.

Avery looked to the shelf and picked up a box of red ones. "How about we use both black and red. You can have your gothic tree on one side and I can have my Santa extravaganza on the other, huh?" he asked.

"Sounds perfect," Davey said sarcastically, although the sarcasm was nothing more than amusement in disguise, and he gave the fact away when he laughed straight after his comment.

Why did it feel as if he'd known Avery his entire life? Why did it feel, even after a fortnight of dating, as if he was hanging out with his best friend?

Walking out on the streets, heading back to Avery's place, Davey noticed the amount of people walking beside them with endless bags balanced in both hands and children wearing Santa hats, singing carols and dragging their parents to every flashing costly object that was on display.

For a change, it didn't disgust him.

For a change it looked cozy.

Manhattan of all places, the streets of it, looked welcoming. Davey had to pinch himself to make sure he was still there and not hallucinating. And the confirmation came when Avery put his arm around Davey's shoulders and kissed the side of his head.

If it was a dream, then he certainly did not wish to wake up.

They rounded the corner to Avery's flat, and Avery's hold loosened before dropping entirely to his side. Davey looked at Avery, who was gazing in the distance. He followed Avery's line of sight and spotted a man outside Avery's front door. Avery's face dropped.

"What's wrong? Who is that?" Davey asked, his stomach clenching as if it was being encased in a tight fist and suspicion curled up to his lungs.

Avery didn't move, nor did his gaze. "That's my ex," he said, and the fist in Davey's stomach clenched tighter, stronger, making him want to fold in two.

"Wh-what's he doing here?" he said after a moment.

"I have no clue," Avery replied and started walking towards the guy.

Davey wasn't sure if he was supposed to follow or stay behind. He wasn't sure what was happening and what made Avery so upset. He decided to chase after Avery and catch up to him.

"I see you wasted no time," the guy told Avery with a smirk in his face.

"What are you doing here?" Avery yelled.

The man ran his fingers through his blonde hair and took joy in the moment. "I just thought I'd visit. Do you not want me here?" he asked.

Avery looked away from him. "You couldn't call?"

"I wanted to talk. In person," he responded, his casualness shrinking away.

Avery still avoided looking at the man. "What could we possibly have to talk about, Kyle?"

Kyle shrugged and looked at Avery again. "Can we—do this inside? It's kinda cold out here," he said.

Davey wasn't sure if he was needed or if he was being a voyeur, standing there between two former lovers who obviously still had feelings for each other, although whether those feelings matched he wasn't so sure about just yet.

"I've got company," Avery said, now daring to look at Kyle in the face.

"I can go," Davey said breathless and composed himself. "I will go."

Avery looked at him. "No, you don't have to."

"It's okay. I'm beat, anyway. I guess I'll see you later," he said and wasn't sure if he should kiss him goodbye or just leave it altogether. He definitely wanted to, but Kyle's stare was burning his face, and he wasn't sure Avery wanted to kiss in front of his ex.

He set off back the way they'd come and climbed down the subway. All the while he tried to imagine all the possible outcomes of what had just happened.

All the while his heart thumped with dread.

———

THE NEXT FEW HOURS WERE A HORROR. HE HAD no way of knowing what was happening downtown at Avery's place and no courage to find out by calling him. What was killing him the most was that he couldn't keep his mind occupied from imaginary scenarios, both good and bad, as he was off work and making picture frames was proving a challenging act.

He watched TV, or had it playing in the background while he attempted to not look at his phone every two seconds. He couldn't eat, his stomach tied up and heavy, and his throat, although parched, couldn't swallow a darned thing.

He made a sport out of opening his messages to find out he had no new ones and then reprimanding himself for being so obsessed over a guy he hardly knew. Then he would play out his desired scenario in his head only to confirm its unlikelihood by looking at his empty messages again.

He was coming out of the washroom when his phone pinged, and he practically ran across the room to fetch it. He opened his messages and was overcome by disappointment when he found out it was a message from his friend Laurie.

As he typed away a response to her *hey*, another ping echoed around the apartment and he opened Avery's message without bothering to finish his first one. It read:

Hey. Sorry about earlier. I did not see that coming. Davey wanted to scream but held his lungs and chords under control. What the hell kind of a message was that, after so many hours of agonizing about him?

Instead of saying so in his message, he typed, *How are you? Want to talk?*

The next moments felt like eons until he received the reply.

I'm busy at the moment. If you don't mind I just need some time to think.

Davey was getting wound up now and he was doing his absolute best to rein it in. *What does that mean?*

Was that too aggressive? Would he be insulted? Then he reminded himself that he shouldn't care what Avery thought, especially if he was about to end whatever they had.

Honestly, I don't even know. I'll call you in a couple of days. I just need to clear my head, he said.

That was it. He was breaking up with him. Not that they were in a relationship to start with, but Davey didn't care. He knew what Avery was doing. He was never the right guy. He was always the wrong size, age, gender, partner. He was never the right one. He was always the rebound or the backup. Never the main guy. Never the one. No matter how many times he thought the other person was his Prince Charming.

He started crying before he could control his emotions. He had no reason to cry other than being rejected again.

When would his time come? When would he get his man and live their happily ever after? Was it childish still waiting for it to happen? The logical part of his brain, the one that kept score of the heartbreak and the heartache, told him a big resounding yes, but the other part of him, the hopeless romantic that he had tried to bury not very successfully, was telling him not to give up. To keep hoping.

And it was with that minuscule hope that he went out, on his couch.

SEVEN

Going to work the next morning was a pain he could feel deep in his bones. He was completely off-balance, so much that he was even early to work because he woke up at sunrise with aching joints and a stiff neck.

There had been no more messages from Avery since the last, and it was almost a relief when he realized he had slept and stopped worrying about a response.

As much as it was a relief, though, there was twice as much worry as he resumed his constant phone checking, even while he was working and ringing items through the till.

During his lunch break he decided to switch off his phone and give himself some space to breathe. It felt rejuvenating. Why was he even so obsessed?

Avery had been in his life for just a couple of weeks. He literally meant nothing to Davey.

Thinking that however, brought a pang of guilt in his chest. Avery was the first guy to ever listen to him and relate. He was the first one to ever take time to know Davey before bedding him. Avery was the first one to look at Davey and see him and not some sex-crazed version of a fuck-buddy. Avery was the first person to feel as much of a friend as much he was a lover. Those eyes, twinkling and grey and so enthralling, and that cheeky smile that could haunt him for hours after.

He put down his paper bag and coffee cup and looked around him. It was cold but also gloomy and dark. He lit up a cigarette and inhaled until his brain buzzed with a headache. It was a welcome distraction from the painful image of Avery in his mind.

He took a sip of his hot eggnog latte and looked around. Couples walked hand in hand, kissing under mistletoes and taking pictures in front of fake snow and Santa grottos.

His chest pummeled with pain. Why couldn't he have this? They all looked so happy, so ecstatic to be in each other's company, no exes creeping up in their relationships. No strange messages to decode. There was pure love around him, and he was unashamedly jealous.

He returned to work twenty minutes later but

turned his phone on before taking his position back. When the screen flashed and loaded he was notified of a new message.

Avery!

He opened it and read. *Hey, handsome. Sorry about yesterday. My brain was fried. Do you want to meet me after work?*

Yes, yes, yes! He wanted to scream and shout and cheer and maybe hop with joy, but he composed himself.

Avery wanted to see him again. He hadn't just disappeared without further communication. He had another chance with this dream of a man. He pinched himself to make sure he wasn't, in fact, dreaming, but it was the reprimanding voice of Emily that made him jump.

"Come on, Davey. You're late. Again!" she said and retreated back in the office.

The rest of the shift was a breeze, and Davey already had a plan.

The minute the clock struck six, he darted past the staff lockers, picked up his stuff, and went browsing through the aisles of the shop in search of the sweater he had spotted while working and craved. It was an emerald green sweater with a mistletoe print sewn on the front. He picked up a matching beanie and gloves and went to the checkout where his colleague rang everything through and scanned his discount card. After he paid, he went in search of the washrooms a floor down, where he changed into his new clothes and stuffed his old clothes into his bag. Having done that, he entered a perfume shop and sprayed himself with a sample of his favorite fragrance, then went out of the mall and rode the subway a couple of stops. When he came out of it, he walked a block to Avery's place. He saw a crowd smoking outside a bar named White Hart Winery and walked in to find Avery standing by the bar with a bottle of beer in his hand.

"Hey, handsome," he said when he saw him. Avery seemed to be in another world but returned to the current one with a kiss.

The music was blaring and the crowd was growing. They were glued to each other, as people attempted to order drinks on either side of them.

"Do you want to get out of here?" Avery asked. "Somewhere quieter?"

Davey nodded and Avery set his beer down and followed Davey back outside. Avery took a deep breath and they walked the streets.

"Where do you want to go?"

Avery shrugged. He seemed pensive.

"What's wrong?"

Avery shook his head. "Nothing. Sorry. My brain still goes back to yesterday."

All the merriment he had felt the entire day, and on his way to meet Avery, evaporated with that single sentence. All the stress and worry returned. They walked in silence for a few moments before Davey took a risk and asked what had happened.

"Well, Kyle came to tell me he wants me back and he regrets breaking up with me. He said he still loves me and so on and so on," Avery said without hesitation.

Maybe he had been practicing that speech the whole day. Maybe the whole reason why he messaged him was to break up with him in person. He couldn't decide if that was crueler or nicer.

"And what did you say?"

Avery looked up to the sky. "I told him I didn't know if it'd be any good to get back together. He thinks he doesn't stand a chance against you."

The suggestion took him by surprise. "What does he have to worry about? We're only dating." It felt strange having that kind of conversation with the man he liked. As if he was trying to justify Kyle's feelings and undermine his.

"I know," was all Avery said.

It wasn't much comfort, and he imagined neither it was for Kyle.

"So, what are you going to do?" Davey asked.

"I don't know," came the answer.

Davey bit his lip and fought with himself. He wanted to beg. He wanted to keep him. But he would never admit that to Avery. Not now. Not like this.

"I—I lied when I said it's been a while since my last relationship," he admitted.

Avery looked at him with a perplexed look. "What do you mean?"

"When we went on our first date, I told you it'd been a while since my last relationship. I lied. The truth is that it had only been a day since I'd broken up with my ex," he said but chose to look away. He couldn't possibly look at those big, wonderful eyes while throwing what they had under the bus.

Avery's stare tickled his face. "O-kay. Why are you telling me this?"

Davey shrugged. "I don't know. I wanted to be honest with you. The truth is I've never had a relationship that lasted more than a couple months. And it's never my fault. I know that of course I would say that, but it's true. I always put the time and effort, the feelings, the emotions, the thought, but *they* always seem to run for the hills," he said. It felt equally liberating and toxic saying it. Liberating to admit it to someone else. Toxic to his sanity.

Avery didn't reply.

"Don't feel guilty. If my ex came to me now, I'd probably get back with him too. You don't have to think about hurting me, if you are at all. I'm a big boy. I can handle it." He wasn't sure if that was true, because his mouth tasted sour saying it. He didn't know how much more heartache he could take before he gave up.

"Don't say that," Avery said, but he wasn't looking at Davey anymore and neither was Davey looking at Avery. They were walking together like two strangers on the same path.

"It's true. Follow your heart, baby," he said, and the word tasted foreign in his mouth.

They walked a couple of more blocks, hardly any words passing between them. He was scared of being the first to step out of the situation, though. He liked to hope. Even though he knew that hope would be crushed to the ground sooner or later.

"I'm sorry for being a lousy company tonight," Avery broke the silence.

Davey shrugged. "It's okay. I'm not always a great company either."

More silence.

"I think I'm gonna go. Sorry for ruining your evening," Avery said. He looked at Davey's eyes with a sadness he hadn't seen before. He wished he could wipe it off.

"You didn't. Really," he lied.

———

THE WALK HOME WAS A PAIN. HIS MIND DIDN'T want to cooperate in keeping him safe. It ignored traffic lights, passerbys and lampposts.

Another pointless relationship. Time wasted,

feelings invested. All for his heart to be shattered, left alone to mend it, yet again.

And all after he promised himself he wouldn't get attached, wouldn't let anyone in again. He had failed himself just as much as someone else had failed him.

He couldn't go on like this. Not for long. He was only twenty-five, and he had been destroyed more times than anyone could have tolerated in a lifetime. Enough was enough.

He got into his apartment, already decided on his next step. He took his shoes off, turned the TV on, and grabbed his phone.

Hey, Avery. I wanted to let you know that going out with you was one of the best times of my life, but if you still have feelings for Kyle and you think there's something still there, you should give him another chance. You guys already have something. We've only just met. Go and be happy, he wrote, his heart feeling twice the size and his breath catching. But he had made himself a promise, and he was going to keep it now more than ever. If the guy didn't want to be with him, he wasn't going to beg.

His finger hovered over the Send button. He closed his eyes and pressed it, letting out a wild scream from his throat before he was enveloped in tears once again.

Just his damn luck. Alone and battered, yet again.

EIGHT

The response never came. The next day he went to work like a zombie that had given up on finding his prey.

He was inconsolable and even though he wouldn't let his feelings show to his colleagues — what did they care anyway? — he was more concerned about his mental stability.

It almost felt as if he'd lost his mother all over again. The pain, the hurt, the hopelessness. And every time he would think this way, he would reprimand himself for comparing the loss of his dear mother with that of losing a man he barely knew.

When he went back home, he picked up a pack of beer on his way in, once again trying to drown his pain in things that could do nothing for it. He wanted to feel nothing. He wanted the ability to be as emotionless as the all the guys he had met who had discarded him as if he was a toy they were bored playing with.

He cracked the beer open when his door bell rang. Who could it possibly be? His friends were out frolicking as usual, never bothering inviting him out, knowing he wouldn't go with them anyway. No one else knew where he lived. No one that mattered anyway.

He opened the door and found Avery standing there with a shy grin and a bouquet of blue carnations. His favorite flowers.

"What—what are you doing here?" He was lost for words. "How did you find me?"

Avery's grin disappeared as he let the bouquet drop to his side. "I got your address from work. It took a lot of convincing and they should probably be charged with something for giving away private information, but it brought me here, so I'm not complaining."

Davey shook his head in confusion. "But, what are you *doing* here?"

"You told me to go be happy. In your message. So, that's what I'm doing."

Davey's legs felt like jelly. Had he heard right?

"And these are for you," he said, passing the bouquet to Davey, who took the flowers from his hands and inhaled their aroma.

"How did you know?"

Avery chuckled. "Nothing a good Facebook stalking won't do," he answered.

"But why?" Davey felt as if his mind was playing tricks on him.

These things didn't happen. These things happen to him, especially. These things happened in movies. These things happened to other people. Not to him. Not to desperate, hopeless romantic Davey. Never him.

"You know yesterday, when you told me about your ex. About your exes. I'm so sorry they never appreciated you, because you're the best human I've met. You're sane, you're logical, you're unique and quirky. You're not the lousy company you think you are. You're the best company I've had." Avery was blushing, and from the heat in Davey's cheeks, he assumed he was too.

"But you're in love with Kyle," he said, trying to bring the man to his senses. Surely, he didn't mean all those things. Those were not words meant for him.

Avery dipped his head. "It's true, I've still got feelings for him. We were together for seven years. I can't just erase how I felt for him. But he still hurt me. He still neglected me and tortured me with his constant judgment of my life. And we never wanted the same things. He caused me so much hurt I could never go back to him."

Davey wanted to cuddle him and never let him

go, but he restrained himself. He had made himself a promise. "But you were considering it. You were thinking about him, yesterday, when we were together," Davey accused him, and he hated himself for it as much as he admired his courage to defend his heart.

Avery shook his hand. "No, that's not what that was. Kyle and I, we had a long conversation. He was trying to remind me all the good times and why we were good together. When I was with you, I was remembering all those things and trying to think of a time that I didn't feel all those things with you, in your company. It was just my brain coming to the realization that I wanted to be with you.

"It was hard to find out that after seven years, I no longer felt the love for the man I'd spent most of my adult life with. But I feel like I've known you my entire life, Davey, and I know there's so many things we don't know about each other, but I still feel like I'm with a friend, a best friend, when I'm with you.

"You make me smile and laugh and you make my heart beat a million times faster when you look at me. I don't want Kyle back. I want to build a future with you," he said and, as an afterthought, added, "if you want that too."

Davey felt hot, way too hot to be encompassed in the small hallway, listening to things he always dreamed of, but never thought would be spoken in in sincerity in real life.

"I would like that, too," he said finally.

Avery took a step forward and leaned closer. His kiss was soft and affectionate. He could feel the need in it, and he hoped he was reciprocating. Because he did need Avery, no matter how much he lied to himself.

When they released each other's lips Davey cupped Avery's face and whispered to him.

"I lied as well. I would never go back to my ex, either. I—feel like a better person when I'm with you. And I also feel as if I've known you for years. My heart does. I think it recognized you from another lifetime the minute I set my eyes on you."

Avery's eyes glimmered solely for his benefit. The trademark cheeky smile made its appearance, and desire was in his eyes.

Avery kissed him again, taking slow steps forward, and closed the door behind him. Davey dropped the bouquet on the floor and took Avery's face in both hands. The kiss deepened, and tongues were reintroduced to each other.

Avery's hands dropped to Davey's hips, and his erection pressed against Davey's.

Davey led Avery to his bedroom, not allowing any room for breath. Only when they reached the bed did he do so, as he pushed Avery on it and fell on top of him.

Davey's hands navigated to Avery's hips and rubbed his hands gently as both their hard-ons ground on each other. Avery moaned in his mouth and Davey shivered with the desire. Avery's hands cupped his butt cheeks and squeezed them before bringing both his hands up to Davey's shoulder blades and holding on to him for dear life.

Davey eased himself out of the tight embrace and went down on Avery, retrieving Avery's cock from beneath the zipper and sucking on the sweet juices the man's erection was already dripping.

Avery pulled Davey's hair, guiding his head and controlling his rhythm. Davey ignored his gag reflex and took the entire length of the man in his mouth before he came up for air and a kiss on the lips. Avery stopped him from going back down on him, instead pulling him down on the mattress and undressing him.

First Avery pulled Davey's sweater off and caressed his chest. Avery sucked on one of his nipples while he undid Davey's trousers' buttons.

Davey took his jeans and boxers off and Avery wasted no time in pleasing him with his wet mouth. Davey relaxed and let his arms rest on his side as the man worked on his erection. He gripped the sheet under his fists, unable to control himself. He came in Avery's mouth before he could warn him, but Avery moaned as he licked Davey's cum and came back up to him for a warm embrace.

They stayed in each other's arms for a long time

before either of them spoke. Avery's heat made Davey's eyes feel heavy. His next memory was the blinding morning light penetrating through his window and finding Avery next to him, naked, asleep and beautiful.

It hadn't been a dream after all. It all had really happened. A man actually chose him over another. He was wanted. And he believed it, for a change. He smiled, and sleep encompassed him once more.

———

WHEN DAVEY OPENED HIS EYES NEXT, AVERY WAS gone. He patted the comforter on the bed and scoped the bedroom, but he wasn't there. So it *had* all been a dream. Why would anything good ever happen to him? Why would he get his happily ever after? He was not made for those. He wasn't a movie or a bestselling book. He was Davey and he was out of luck. Forever.

He heard a thump from the other room and he jumped out of bed, half in terror of what might that be and half hopeful. Still. Even after all that had happened to him. He entered the living room, and the relief showered him with shivers throughout his entire body.

It had not been a dream. Avery was standing in front of a shelf, inspecting one of Davey's frames. A steamy mug was resting on the shelf. Possibly the source of the thump he had heard. Avery sensed Davey behind him and turned to face him with a smile.

"Good morning, handsome," he said.

It sounded like music in Davey's ears. His luck had turned around. Avery had come to him, confessing his feelings for him, professing his interest in the weirdo that he was. He had not scared Avery away and neither had Avery chosen to let Davey go for someone else. Avery was his and Davey was Avery's. He still couldn't understand how his luck had changed so suddenly. It was like…

It was like a Christmas miracle, and he didn't even believe in those. But Avery was the living proof standing in front of him.

"Hey," he responded and embraced the man of his dreams.

"You want some coffee?" Avery asked. "Sorry for taking the liberty to make my own cup, but I can't function without it in the morning," he said, pulling back and staring into Davey's eyes.

Davey smiled. "It's okay. And yes, some coffee would be great."

Avery walked to the kitchen and opened the cupboards in search of a mug and the ingredients required.

"What were you doing?" Davey asked him,

taking the frame Avery had been inspecting earlier and looking for clues.

Avery smirked. "Well, you told me you make frames, but I'd never actually seen them before. I was just looking at what you've made. They are wonderful."

"They're nonsense," Davey answered automatically.

"You've got a talent," Avery said. Davey wasn't sure if he'd heard him and ignored his comment, or not heard him at all while making him a cup of coffee. "It's a shame they're empty, though," he said and he approached Davey with a cup of steam. The smell of the brew hit his nostrils, and his eyes widened as if in response to the strong caffeine.

"I told you." Davey took the cup in his hands. "I don't have any pictures left. All of them, along with my memories, were thrown away," he answered.

Avery eased himself into an embrace and squeezed Davey's shoulder blades with affection. "Let's make some new ones, then."

Avery reached for his back pocket and when he lifted his hand, it was holding his phone. He stretched his hand to fit both of them in the camera's frame and snapped a few shots. He then proceeded to review the pictures with Davey.

"I like this one," Davey said.

"Me too. Let's print it when we're out. Then we

can start filling these in," he said and waved at the shelf full of frames.

Davey took a deep breath. Yep. Definitely a Christmas miracle. "I'd like that very much," he said and kissed Avery.

NINE

All I want for Christmas, is you chimed on the radio, and Davey wiggled his hips to the rhythm of the all-time bore of a song of the season. He no longer cared. He had all he could ever ask for. He had Avery. And he was more than enough for Davey.

He took the chicken out of the oven and placed it on the stovetop, then refilled his glass with a fine red Montepulciano. He was singing along to the song when he felt Avery's crotch rubbing on his buttocks, and Davey took him in his embrace, dancing along with him.

"Dinner is almost ready," Davey said.

"And so is my surprise," Avery said.

He had asked Davey to stay in the kitchen and not come out until Avery told him so. Davey was happy to oblige, considering he had so much to prepare before they could sit down and enjoy their Christmas meal. Davey made to go out of the kitchen, but Avery's hand blocked his way.

"Not yet. Let's plate the dinner first. I'm hungry," he said.

Davey obeyed and carved the chicken into thin slices, spooning the stuffing onto the plate and stocking it up with the roasted vegetables he had been working on the whole day.

"You know? When you suggested we go for chicken instead of turkey, I thought you were crazy, but seeing this, I don't even know how the two of us would handle a whole turkey," Avery said. When he saw the finished meal on the plate, with the gravy and the cranberry sauce, it looked like twice as much as what they could actually have.

"Well, I'm clever that way," Davey replied and danced around Avery, taking the two plates with him and finally gaining access to the living room, where the dining table had been set by Avery. When he put the plates on their placemats, he realized that something other than the table looked different.

Avery was right behind him, looking at the shelf as well. All of the frames had been filled with pictures, their pictures. The ones they had managed to take in a span of two weeks.

They had only met three weeks ago, but it

already felt like a lifetime spent in happiness and bliss. There were pictures of them from the skating rink that Davey had actually dreaded visiting.

Snaps of them at the karaoke after a night of one too many drinks.

One of their visit to the Smithsonian, and them dressed in warm clothes at the Rockefeller Center in front of the Christmas tree.

It had only been three weeks, but the shelf was already full of memories.

"That's…" Davey was lost for words. He never thought he'd have any of this.

"I know," Avery whispered.

"I'm happy," Davey said.

"I'm the happiest I've ever been," Avery said.

Davey kissed him. The kiss was full of love and passion.

"I love you," he murmured between their lips.

"I love you too," Avery said.

And it was true. Impossible as it sounded, they had found love and they were happy in such a short time.

He didn't even know what the rest of their life together would be like if the beginning was so perfect. He couldn't wait to find out.

———

WANT TO FIND OUT WHAT HAPPENS NEXT IN Davey and Avery's life?

Check out my bonus epilogue called "A Memory to be Made" by clicking here.

A LETTER FROM RHYS

I wrote this a few years back but it still holds a special place in my heart.

You see it was inspired by how I met my now-husband and the whirlwind of an insta-love romance we had.

I'm not going to go into details about what's accurate and what isn't. I wouldn't want to ruin the fiction of it all, or get too personal.

I will say this however.

The scarf thing? When Avery offers it to Davey to protect him from the cold. That really happened. And the conversation around it. "You'll have to meet me to give it back to me."

And that was my way of manipulating him so that he *had* to meet me again since he had my scarf.

I hope you enjoyed this story, even though it's a

little different to my usual ordeal, very low on heat, written in third person and quite short.

And if this is your first foray into my books, why not check out my other books?

I've got something for everyone.

Don't forget to leave a review if you have a spare minute. and catch you in our next happily-ever-after.

Rhys Everly
September 2021

ALSO BY RHYS

For the most up-to-date list, visit
rhyswritesromance.com/books

RHYS EVERLY

Sexy romance with all the feels

CEDARWOOD BEACH SERIES:

Fresh Start, Book 1

Wayward Love, Book 2

Rogue Affair, Book 3

Storm Bound, Book 4

Royal Fling, Book 5

A PROPER EDUCATION SERIES:

Beau Pair

Me Three

Your Only Fan

Missing Linc

STANDALONES

Street Love (A hurt/comfort romance) (Also available in
Italian)

Hair and Heart (A Rapunzel Retelling)

AUDIOBOOKS

My books are coming in audio. For an up-to-date list
visit my website at rhyswritesromance.com/audio

RHYS EVERLY

Sexy romance with all the feels

CEDARWOOD BEACH SERIES

NARRATED BY NICK HUDSON

Fresh Start, Book 1

A PROPER EDUCATION SERIES

NARRATED BY JOHN YORK

Teach for Treat

Beau Pair

———

RHYS LAWLESS

Killer romance. One spell at a time.

CURSED HEARTS SERIES:

NARRATED BY JOHN YORK

Killer Heart, Book 1

ABOUT THE AUTHOR

Rhys Everly-Lawless is a hopeless romantic who loves happily-ever-afters.

Which would explain why he loves writing them.

When he's not passionately typing out his next book, you can find him cuddling his dog, feeding his husband, or taking long walks letting those plot bunnies breed ferociously in his head.

He writes contemporary gay romances as Rhys Everly and LGBTQ+ urban fantasy and paranormal romances as Rhys Lawless.

You can find out more about him and his works-in-progress by joining his Facebook group or visiting his website rhyswritesromance.com

Printed in Great Britain
by Amazon